for Simon Lindley
and the choir of St Alban's Scho

GW00471405

Donkey Ca

Allegretto comodo e grazioso (♪ = c.184)

PIANO

mf

dim.

Verse 1 SOPRANOS
mf Verse 2 TENORS

1. Don - key rid - ing o - ver the bum - py road,_____
2. Don - key watch - ing o - ver the Je - sus child,_____

Ww. (2nd time)

2nd time

mp

Car - ry Ma - ry, all with her hea - vy load;_____
See the ba - by, all with his mo - ther mild;_____

This carol is scored for double woodwind, 2 horns, percussion, harp, and strings. Scores and parts are on hire.

A version for two-part voices is also on sale (T111).

V.1 TENORS
V.2 SOPRANOS

Fol - low Jo - seph, lead - ing you on your way Un - til you
Hear the an - gels sing - ing their song on high: 'No - well, no -

find a sta - ble, some - where to rest and stay._____
- well, no - well', their ca - rol - ling fills the sky._____

SOPRANOS and TENORS

Don - key rid - ing o - ver the bum - py road,_____
Don - key watch - ing o - ver the Je - sus child,_____

3. Donkey resting all in a manger stall,____

(Hum)

(Hum)

(Hum)

With the ox - en wor-ship the Lord of all.____

Hush, he lies a - sleep on his bed of hay While Ma - ry

lul - la - lay.'

sings so sweet - ly 'Lul - la, lul - la,_____ lul - la, lul - la -

poco rall.

accel.

wor - ship the Lord of____ all.____

cresc.

C a tempo

mf

SOPRANOS

TENORS

4. Don - key wak - ing all at the break of day,

Ah

See, a new light shin - ing with bright - est

Ah

ray, Long the wea - ry

12

S. -well, no - well, no - well, no - well, no - well, no - well, no -

A.
T.
B. way; _____ Al - le - lu - - ia,

-well, no - well, no - well, no - well. Ding - a - dong, ding dong,

Je - sus is born to - day. _____ Hark, the